ISBN 978-1-4847-2088-2
FAC-023680-18211
3 5 7 9 10 8 6 4

MICKEY'S
SURPRISE BIRTHDAY

Disney PRESS

New York • Los Angeles

Mickey woke up and jumped out of bed. As he slipped his feet into his slippers, he said good morning.

Mickey ate his breakfast, like he did every day. He brushed his teeth, like he did every day. And he did his stretches, like he did every day. But today was not like every other day.

Today was Mickey's birthday!

"What should we do today?" Mickey asked Pluto.

But Pluto wasn't paying attention to Mickey. He was staring out the window.

Mickey looked out the window, too. His friends were walking along the path behind his house.

I wonder what they're doing, Mickey thought.

Mickey looked closer. Donald was carrying cups and plates. Daisy was carrying lemonade. Goofy was carrying a bunch of balloons. And Minnie was carrying a big cake.

"Pluto!" Mickey shouted. "It looks like they're having a party!"

Mickey looked out the window again. "Do you think they know it's my birthday? Could they be having a birthday party . . . for me?"

"We'd better get dressed, Pluto," Mickey said. "Just in case!"

So Mickey dusted off his gloves and polished his buttons.
He even brushed Pluto.

Soon they were ready.

Mickey and Pluto sat in the living room and waited for their
friends. And waited . . . and waited. But no one came.

Finally, the doorbell rang. Mickey jumped up and raced to the door. He threw it open, ready for his party. But there was no party outside. There was only Donald. And he looked upset.

"What's wrong, Donald?" Mickey asked.

"My favorite hammock is broken," Donald told Mickey. "I can't nap without it! Can you help me fix it?"

So Donald, Mickey, and Pluto set off to fix the hammock. As they walked, an idea popped into Mickey's head.

Maybe there is no broken hammock, he thought. Maybe Donald is really taking me to my party!

Mickey was so excited that he started to skip.

Donald led Mickey into his front yard. He stopped in front of
two trees and looked down. There, on the ground, was the broken
hammock.

Mickey looked around. There were no balloons and no cake.
There was just one friend who needed his help. So Mickey helped
Donald fix his hammock.

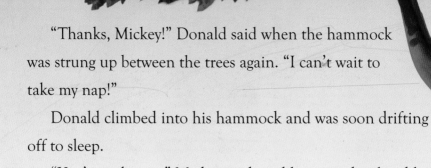

"Thanks, Mickey!" Donald said when the hammock was strung up between the trees again. "I can't wait to take my nap!"

Donald climbed into his hammock and was soon drifting off to sleep.

"You're welcome," Mickey said, and he started to head home.

I guess there wasn't a party after all, Mickey thought as he walked. Just then, he heard Minnie and Daisy calling him.

"Mickey," Minnie said. "We have something to show you!"

"Just wait 'til you see it!" Daisy said.

So Mickey went with Minnie and Daisy. As he walked, Mickey began to wonder about a party again.

Maybe they are taking me to my party! he thought.

Minnie and Daisy led Mickey to their flower garden.

"Ta-da!" said Daisy.

"Everything is blooming!" said Minnie.

"Do you want to help us garden?" Minnie asked.

Mickey thought about it. He didn't have any other plans.

And so he helped water the flowers.

A few minutes later, Goofy ran up and pulled Mickey away.

"Mickey! Mickey!" Goofy shouted, tugging on his friend's arm.
"You've got to see this. I've never seen anything like it!"

Mickey waved good-bye to Minnie and Daisy and rushed away
with Goofy.

Goofy seems very excited, Mickey thought as his friend rushed him down the road. I wonder what he wants to show me.

Then Mickey realized, Goofy must be taking him to his party! Suddenly, Goofy stopped running.

"Look, Mickey," he said, pointing to a large rock.

Mickey looked all around, but there was no sign of a party. Why was Goofy so excited?

Then Mickey looked down. Two snails were racing on the rock.

"Gosh! Watch 'em go!" Goofy said. "Have you ever seen anything so exciting?"

Mickey had never seen a snail race before. It was interesting, but he wasn't sure it was exciting!

It definitely wasn't as exciting as a party!

Mickey and Pluto watched the snails race for a while. Then they headed home.

"Oh, well, Pluto," Mickey said. "I guess I was wrong."

Pluto whimpered. He had never seen Mickey look so sad.

Mickey walked up the path to his house. He opened the front door and stepped inside.

As he reached for the light switch . . .

Surprise! Mickey's friends jumped out at him. They had planned a party after all. A surprise party! For the first time all day, Mickey had not expected it.

"I don't understand," he said. "I thought you were all busy today. How did find time to plan a party . . . at my house . . . without me finding out?"

Mickey thought about his day. . . . Donald's broken hammock
. . . Daisy and Minnie's flowers . . . Goofy's snail race.

Now Mickey understood. Mickey smiled a huge smile. He was
glad his friends had tricked him. He loved surprise parties!

"Thanks, everyone," Mickey said, "for the best party ever!"